Pelican's Lemons

Written by Riya Aarini

Illustrated by Mariana Hnatenko

To those who make life a little sweeter with lemonade.

- RA

Text copyright © 2022 by Riya Aarini

Illustrations by Mariana Hnatenko

ISBN: 978-1-956496-00-0 (Hardcover)

ISBN: 978-1-956496-01-7 (Paperback)

ISBN: 978-1-956496-02-4 (eBook)

Library of Congress Control Number: 2021921747

First published in Chicago, Illinois, USA

Visit www.riyapresents.com

Welcome to Welican,
An isle of pelicans.

Young Nelican flapped his wings.
The pelican stretched with glee!
He lived on a sandy beach
On Welican's breezy sea!

The Welican sun rose high.
The fireball glistened bright.
He fancied the splendid morn
And wanted to fish for a bite.

He opened the cracked front door.

The porch held a strange new scene.

Inside an old wooden crate

Were lemons—and some still green!

The fruit had arrived in a flash.

Bewildered, he asked, "What's this?"

He stared at the great surprise,

A sight that he couldn't miss!

Now lemons were really odd
For pelicans on the isle.
Though Nelican had no plan
He brought them inside with a smile.

"I've stumbled on plenty here.
There's three in this lemon bed.
I count at least twenty more!
That's twenty-three fruits," he said.

He juggled the lemons high.
The pelican really tried!
In seconds, the fruits crashed down.
Dazed Nelican lost his pride.

Inside his gigantic pouch,
He dropped the fruits one by one.
"These lemons are sour!" he wailed
And puckered like a hot cross bun!

The bundle of baffling fruit,
Just then the wise pelican knew,
Was trouble to say the least.
But handing them out might do!

Tough Pelican Joe was first.

Brave Nelican asked, "Fruit, mate?"

Joe mightily shouted, "No!"

And right away slammed the gate.

Then Nelican went to Ann.
She hadn't a thing to say!

She glanced at the loaded crate,
Then shooed the poor bird away!

Dear Nelican carried his fruit
From one front door to the next.
Not one of the neighbors he knew
Had wanted his lemons yet!

"These lemons are useless to me,"
Said Nelican, feeling down.

He dragged all his lemons home
And wore a long pelican frown.

He dropped his enormous load
And shook his tired pelican head.
He didn't know what to do
And wearily crawled to bed.

The fruits were strewn everywhere!
He felt he was hopelessly stuck.

Amidst all the ballyhoo,
He silently wished for luck.

How best to deal with the worst?
Upset, he looked for a clue.
He walked to the kitchen, glum.
There's *one thing* that he could do!

His cabinet held a jug.
He jiggled a wooden spoon.
He noticed a sugar jar.
The cuckoo bird chirped at noon!

He ruffled his feathers clean.
He squeezed the fruit like a ball.
The juice dribbled down at once.
His jug quickly caught it all!

The juice was too bitter to start.
But sugar could make it sweet.
He tossed in twelve sugar cubes
And said, "This will be a treat!"

Smart Nelican stirred the mix.
He added a big lemon slice.
The bright yellow liquid swirled!
He dropped in ten cubes of ice.

He poured the juice from the jug.

The pelican took a taste.

He licked his wide beak and said,

"My trouble won't go to waste!"

Good Nelican grabbed the jug
And nestled beneath the shade.
He called all his pelican pals
For cool homemade lemonade.

The pelicans slurped the drink,
Enjoying the fresh-squeezed juice.
Not one of them made a stink
But gaily danced and let loose!

"What luck!" said tough Pelican Joe.
"Delish!" said delighted Ann.
"How yummy!" they all agreed.
The juice was in high demand!

The pelicans happily sipped
And danced 'til the day was done.
They thanked clever Nelican twice
For bringing joy to everyone!

Nelican's Lemonade

Ingredients:

1 cup freshly squeezed lemon juice (5 to 8 lemons)
1 cup sugar (48 sugar cubes)
5 cups cold water
10 ice cubes
1 big lemon slice

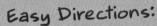

Easy Directions:

Step 1: In a large pitcher, mix the lemon juice, sugar, and water.
Step 2: Stir the lemonade until the sugar dissolves.
Step 3: Toss in ice cubes.
Step 4: Add the lemon slice.
Step 5: Pour into glasses, and share with everyone!

When life leaves a load of
Sour lemony lemons
Stir up lemonade and
Start the celebrations!

Thank you for reading *Nelican's Lemons*!
If you were amused by this story, please consider leaving a review and help other readers discover entertaining picture books.

Children's Books by Riya Aarini
Bella the Terrible
The Country Bake-Off
Cole and the Giant Gingerbread House
Collector of Things & Other Poems
The Veggie Patch Bandits
Pickerton's Jiggle
Ollie's Garden
Ollie's Haffiness

Visit www.riyapresents.com